This Little Tiger book belongs to:

_____

_____

_____

In memory of Nana and Pop
~ C F

To Ellie and Bethany with love
~ R T

LITTLE TIGER PRESS
1 The Coda Centre, 189 Munster Road,
London SW6 6AW
www.littletigerpress.com

First published in Great Britain 2003
This edition published 2003

ISBN 978-1-85430-844-3

A CIP catalogue record for this book is available
from the British Library

Printed in China

4 6 8 10 9 7 5 3

Goodnight, Sleep Tight!

Claire Freedman

Rory Tyger

LITTLE TIGER PRESS
London

One night, Grandma
was looking after Archie.

"Aren't you sleepy yet,
Archie?" asked Grandma.

"No!" replied Archie. "I don't
feel sleepy at all. I'm wide
awake!"

Grandma sat down on the
edge of Archie's bed.

"Have you got all your
favourite friends to cuddle up
with?" she asked. "They might
help you feel sleepy."

"I've got Tiger and Rabbit,"
said Archie. "But where's
Elephant?"

"Here he is," said Grandma,
tucking him in nice and snug.
"You cuddle up and you'll soon
feel sleepy."

But neither Archie nor
his little friends went
to sleep.

"We're still wide
awake, Grandma," he said.

"What about a nice warm
milky drink?" said Grandma.
"That makes me sleepy."

Archie drank every
drop of his warm milk.
But he didn't feel sleepy.
"I'm still wide awake,
Grandma!" he said.
"Please can we watch
the fireflies? That might
make me sleepy."

Grandma wrapped Archie in his cosy
blanket and together they watched the
dancing fireflies. Archie tried to count them
but it didn't make him feel sleepy.

"I'm still wide awake, Grandma!" he said.
"Can you sing me a lullaby, please? That
might make me sleepy."

Grandma sang some of
Archie's favourite songs.
Archie closed his eyes and listened . . .
but he didn't feel sleepy.

"I'm still wide awake, Grandma,"
he whispered.

"I know, Archie," Grandma said.
"Let me rock you in my arms. That
will make you sleepy."

Grandma rocked Archie gently in her arms, all the way down to the apple garden and back. Archie felt safe and warm in Grandma's arms, but he didn't feel the tiniest bit sleepy.

"Grandma, I'm STILL wide awake!" he said. "Will you tell me a story, please? Listening to stories makes me feel sleepy."

Grandma sat down comfortably, and
Archie snuggled up close to her.

She told him stories about all the naughty things his mummy had done when she was little – just like him.

"Your mummy never felt sleepy at bedtime either," Grandma said.

Grandma carried Archie back inside.
She smiled a secret smile as she
remembered putting Archie's
mummy to bed when she
was little.

Grandma tucked Archie up in bed. She pulled the covers right up to his nose.

"I used to tuck your mummy up in bed, with the blankets pulled right up to her nose – like this!" said Grandma.

"Then I'd stroke
the top of
Mummy's
forehead
– like this,"
Grandma said.

Very gently she
stroked the top of Archie's forehead.

"And I'd give Mummy a very special
goodnight kiss," said Grandma.

Grandma gave
Archie a special
goodnight
kiss.

"That's right, Grandma," said Archie
with a big yawn. "And then she says,
'Goodnight, sleep tight!'"
　　"That's right, Archie," said Grandma . . .

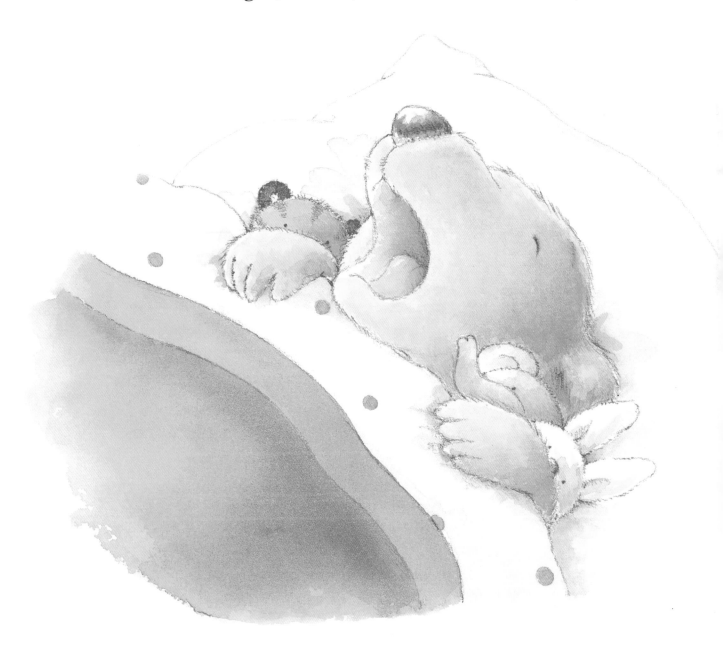

And before Grandma could even say
"Goodnight, sleep tight", Archie was
fast asleep!